Dear Parent:
Your child's love of reading starts here!

Every child learns to read in a different way and at his or her own speed. Some go back and forth between reading levels and read favorite books again and again. Others read through each level in order. You can help your young reader improve and become more confident by encouraging his or her own interests and abilities. From books your child reads with you to the first books he or she reads alone, there are I Can Read Books for every stage of reading:

SHARED READING
Basic language, word repetition, and whimsical illustrations, ideal for sharing with your emergent reader

BEGINNING READING
Short sentences, familiar words, and simple concepts for children eager to read on their own

READING WITH HELP
Engaging stories, longer sentences, and language play for developing readers

READING ALONE
Complex plots, challenging vocabulary, and high-interest topics for the independent reader

ADVANCED READING
Short paragraphs, chapters, and exciting themes for the perfect bridge to chapter books

I Can Read Books have introduced children to the joy of reading since 1957. Featuring award-winning authors and illustrators and a fabulous cast of beloved characters, I Can Read Books set the standard for beginning readers.

A lifetime of discovery begins with the magical words "I Can Read!"

Visit www.icanread.com for information
on enriching your child's reading experience.

To Gracie Anne,
new kid on the block
—K.P.

To Ellie, Jesse, and Emily
—L.C.

HarperCollins®, 🐷®, and I Can Read Book® are trademarks of HarperCollins Publishers Inc.

Library of Congress Cataloging-in-Publication Data
Platt, Kin.
   Big Max and the mystery of the missing giraffe / by Kin Platt ; pictures by Lynne Cravath. —1st ed.
      p.   cm. — (An I Can Read Book)
   Summary: Big Max, the world's greatest detective, must travel to the land of Ah-Ah-Achoo to find the king's missing pet giraffe.
   ISBN-10: 0-06-009918-6 (trade bdg.) — ISBN-13: 978-0-06-00918-3 (trade bdg.)
   ISBN-10: 0-06-009919-4 (lib. bdg.) — ISBN-13: 978-0-06-009919-0 (lib. bdg.)
   ISBN-10: 0-06-009920-8 (pbk. bdg.) — ISBN-13: 978-0-06-009920-6 (pbk. bdg.)
   [1. Giraffe—Fiction.   2. Mystery and detective stories.]   I. Cravath, Lynne Woodcock, ill.   II. Title.   III. Series.
PZ7.P7125Bie   2005   2004006084
[Fic]—dc22   CIP
                                                                                                                    AC

I Can Read!

2
READING WITH HELP

BIG MAX
AND THE MYSTERY OF THE MISSING
GIRAFFE

by **KIN PLATT**   pictures by **LYNNE CRAVATH**
in the style of Robert Lopshire

HarperCollinsPublishers

Big Max was looking out his window.

"It is a nice day for a mystery,"

he said.

The telephone buzzed.

"Ha!" Big Max said.

"Perhaps somebody needs me now."

"Is this Big Max,

the world's greatest detective?"

a voice said.

"I try to be," said Big Max.

"Who is calling, please?"

"This is King Punchapillow.
I am calling from my palace
in Ah-Ah Achoo," the voice said.
"Do you have a cold?" asked Big Max.

7

"No," said the king.

"I've just been stuck

with a lot of silly names."

"What is the problem?"

Big Max asked.

"My pet giraffe, Jake, is missing,"

the king said.

"Can you find him?"

"I can find anything," Big Max said.

"Where is Ah-Ah Achoo?"

9

"It is near some trees," the king said.

"What else is it near?" asked Big Max.

"It is between Sneeze and Gesundheit, just past Runnynose," the king said.

"Do not worry," said Big Max.

"I will be there right away."

"What airline are you taking?"
the king asked.

"My own," said Big Max.

"I fly by umbrella."

11

Big Max blew into his umbrella.

The umbrella filled with air.

"Ready for takeoff," Big Max said.

He flew into the sky.

Big Max flew over the ocean.

He saw a big fish jump.

Big Max flew lower.

"Pardon me," he said.

"Is Runnynose hard to find?"

"Not for whales like me," the fish said.

The whale blew a spout of water.

It splashed over his head.

"See?" the whale said.

"It's not hard."

"Thank you," Big Max said.

"That's a good trick."

Big Max flew over the desert.

"I see camels," he said.

"But no giraffe."

Big Max flew over trees.

Soon he saw a baby deer.

"Pardon me," Big Max said.

"Is this the way to Sneeze?"

"Sorry, I can't help you," the deer said.

"I'm too young.

I don't know how to sneeze yet."

Big Max flew over some more trees.

"I better find it soon," he said.

"I'm running out of air."

The umbrella and Big Max flew lower.

"Prepare for landing!" he shouted.

Big Max landed in a tree.

He stopped falling.

Instead, he started bouncing.

He bounced up and down.

"This is a funny kind of tree,"

Big Max said.

Big Max fell to the ground.

A man came running up.

"Are you Big Max?" he asked.

"I am King Punchapillow."

"This is a funny kind of tree,"
Big Max said.

"It bounces you all around."

"It is supposed to do that,"
the king said. "It is a rubber tree."

"Hm," said Big Max. "Rubber trees
have the rubber stuff inside.
This one has it all over."

"Of course," the king said,
"it is our special kind of rubber tree.
It grows only in Ah-Ah Achoo."

"Hm," said Big Max.

"That is interesting.

Now please show me where

you last saw Jake, your giraffe."

"I hope you can find him,"

the king said.

"I always find what I look for,"

Big Max said.

"I will find him."

The king led Big Max to his palace.

Suddenly the air was filled with sounds.

There were loud roars.

There were loud animal growls.

"Those are wild animal sounds,"

Big Max said.

King Punchapillow smiled.

"Yes," he said.

"But these animals here are not so wild.

They are my pets."

"See?" the king said.

"They are just playing games.

I showed them how to play."

"That is wonderful," Big Max said.

He saw two lions playing ping-pong.

He saw two kangaroos playing tennis.

He saw two bears roller-skating.

"I see two of every kind," said Big Max.

"How many giraffes do you have?"

"Jake was my only giraffe,"

the king said.

"He had nobody to play with.

So I made a place for him

where he could play by himself."

"Show it to me," said Big Max.

The king took Big Max away

to a big courtyard.

Inside was a basketball court.

"See?" the king said.

"He could shoot baskets here

all by himself."

"Hm," said Big Max.

29

"Giraffes don't have hands,"

said Big Max.

"How could Jake shoot baskets?"

"With his mouth," the king said.

"He could blow them in."

"What would Jake do if he missed?"

Big Max asked.

"He would get very mad," said the king.

"What would he do then?" asked Big Max.

"He would kick rocks," said the king.

"When was the last time you saw Jake?"
Big Max asked.

"Last Friday night," the king said.

"We were watching

a soccer game on TV.

The next morning he was gone."

Big Max looked up at the high walls.

"Hm," he said.

"A giraffe cannot jump that high."

He looked closer.

"Giraffes cannot climb walls," he said.

He looked at the lock on the gate.

"Was this gate locked?" Big Max asked.

"Yes, and I have the key," the king said.

"Hm," said Big Max.

"Jake has found a new way

to be missing."

"Perhaps you are not

such a great detective

after all," the king said.

"We shall see," said Big Max.

"Look and think," he said.

"That is the secret to solving a mystery."

"I think we will never find Jake,"

the king said.

"We will find him," Big Max said.

"A giraffe is too big to hide."

Big Max looked up.

"These walls are very high," he said.

"But giraffes are very tall.

Giraffes have long necks.

Jake could look over the walls."

"Yes, he could," said the king.

"But there is nothing to see."

"What is outside the walls?"

asked Big Max.

"Just the trees," the king said.

"My rubber trees."

"Ha!" Big Max said.

"I know how Jake did it!

We must hurry to find him!"

They ran outside.

They ran around the high walls.

They ran around the trees.

"If we find out where Jake went,"

Big Max said,

"we will know why he went."

"I see," said the king.

"Giraffes have big feet," Big Max said.

"These must be Jake's footprints."

"Jake had very big feet," the king said.

"That's why he was good

at kicking rocks."

They followed Jake's tracks.

"If we find out where Jake went,
we will know *why* he went,"
Big Max said.

"Jake never even said good-bye,"
said the king.

"Perhaps he was in a hurry,"
said Big Max.

Suddenly the tracks disappeared.

There was only grass now.

"We have lost the trail," Big Max said.

"Jake, this is not funny,"
the king shouted.

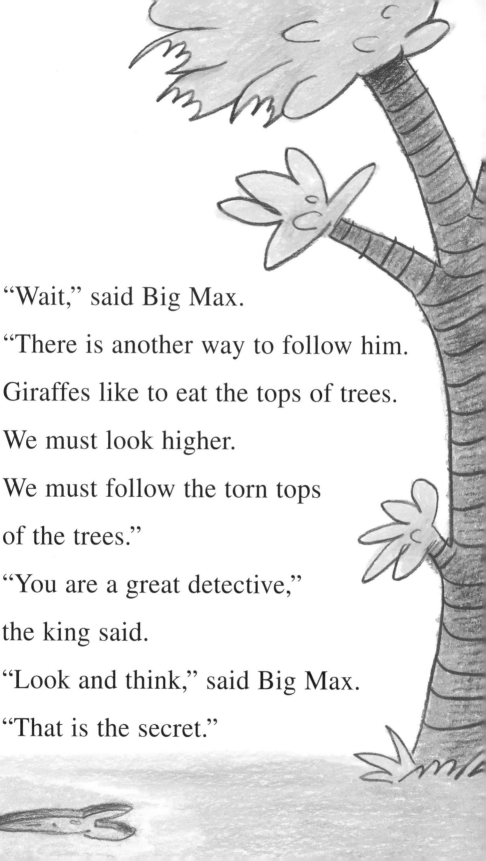

"Wait," said Big Max.

"There is another way to follow him.

Giraffes like to eat the tops of trees.

We must look higher.

We must follow the torn tops

of the trees."

"You are a great detective,"

the king said.

"Look and think," said Big Max.

"That is the secret."

They came to a little stream.

They waded across the water.

They walked up a hill.

Big Max stopped.

"Wait!" he said.

"Why are we stopping?" the king asked.

"Something is wrong," Big Max said.

"This is a different kind of hill," he said.

"This hill is moving.

Hills do not move.

It has thick skin. It has small ears.

It has big teeth like a hippopotamus.

It has the big mouth of a hippopotamus.

So it must be a hippopotamus!"

"I always wondered what I was,"

the hippo said.

"See? I was right!" said Big Max.

"We are looking for a missing giraffe,"
he said.

"Have you seen one?"

"No," the hippo said.

"But you can look inside

and see for yourself."

"No, thank you," Big Max said.

"We will take your word for it."

They hurried away.

There was a great roaring noise.

The ground shook.

The trees shook.

Big Max and the king shook.

"It is an earthquake," the king shouted.

"We must run for our lives!"

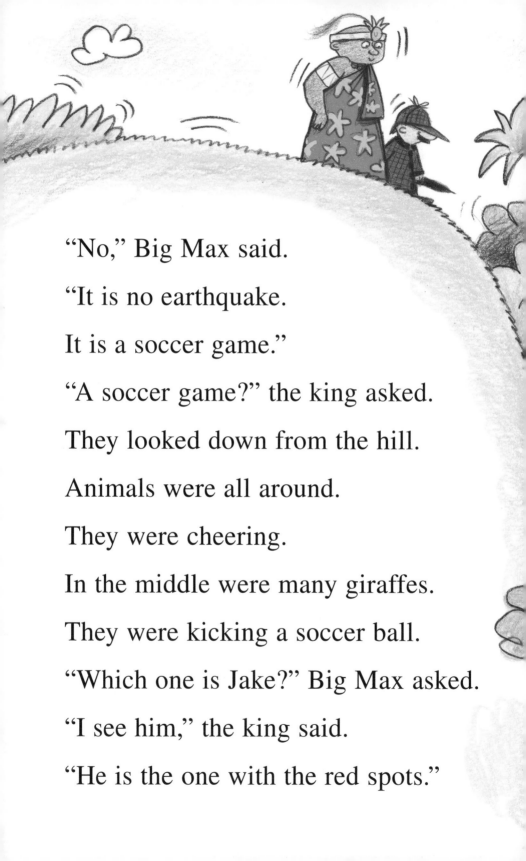

"No," Big Max said.

"It is no earthquake.

It is a soccer game."

"A soccer game?" the king asked.

They looked down from the hill.

Animals were all around.

They were cheering.

In the middle were many giraffes.

They were kicking a soccer ball.

"Which one is Jake?" Big Max asked.

"I see him," the king said.

"He is the one with the red spots."

"Another case solved," Big Max said.

"Now we know why Jake ran away.

When he saw the soccer game on TV,

it reminded him how he missed playing

with his old team."

"No wonder he was always

kicking rocks," the king said.

"He was staying in shape."

"Now I know why Jake ran away,"
said the king.
"What I want to know is,
how did Jake get away?"
"It was the trees," Big Max said.
"It was your special rubber trees.
That was the clue."

Somebody blew a whistle.

"The first half is over," Big Max said.

"Jake will be here soon.

You can ask him yourself."

"Tell me now," the king said.

"I cannot wait that long."

Big Max saw a giraffe coming.

He had red spots all over him.

"Giraffes like to eat leaves,"
Big Max said.
"Jake reached over the wall to chew
the rubber tree leaves.
Rubber stretches. It also snaps back.
It is like pulling on a rubber band.
Jake would pull down a mouthful
of the leaves.
They would stretch back.
The harder Jake pulled,
the harder they stretched back.
Finally, Jake pulled too hard.

The leaves and the rubber branches
pulled back twice as hard.
They pulled Jake over the wall."

"I heard what you said," Jake said.

"Yes, that is how I did it.

That is the first time

I ever liked rubber leaves."

"I'm sorry, Jake," the king said.

"I didn't know

you liked playing soccer."

"It's more fun than kicking rocks,"

Jake said.

The king took out his checkbook.

"How would you like

a million Achoo rupees

for finding Jake?" he said.

"If it's all right with you," Big Max said,

"you can buy us two tickets

for the rest of the game instead.

They just played the first half."

"It's all right with me," said the king.

They watched the soccer game.

Jake's team won 32 to 4.

Big Max said good-bye

to Jake and the king.

Then he blew into his umbrella.

"All's well that ends well," he said.

And off flew Big Max,

the greatest detective in the world.